THE CHILDREN'S
Classic
POETRY
COLLECTION

From friends at
Robert Half Canada
August '99

INTRODUCTION

Poems are magic. In just a few words, they can take you on a journey to a faraway land, or into another person's head! A poem can put even the most difficult feelings into words, or show you a well known object or idea in a completely different way. And the magic of very good poems never ends. Each time you read them, they show you more.

No one really knows how the magic of poems works. After all, they are just made of words. Everything you say or write uses words, but poets use them in a special way. They pay careful attention not only to what a word means, but to how it sounds, too. Some poems seem to beg to be read out loud, so that their words come rolling out of your mouth, making their own music. In poems, words really do become 'rich and strange'.

You may notice that sometimes the poet has used spelling and punctuation that seem odd. That may be because the poem was written long ago or in another country, or the poet may want you to pronounce the words in a special way and only pause for breath in certain places!

The poems in this book have been enjoyed for many years, but the world of poetry is wide and wonderful. I hope you will always find it a magical place to explore.

N.M.A.B.

THE CHILDREN'S
Classic
POETRY
COLLECTION

Compiled by
NICOLA BAXTER

Illustrated by
CATHIE SHUTTLEWORTH

PROSPERO
B·O·O·K·S
A DIVISION OF CHAPTERS INC.

FOR DORA

C.A.S.

This edition published in Canada in 1997
by Prospero Books
A division of Chapters Inc.
90 Ronson Drive, Etobicoke,
Ontario, Canada M9W 1C1.

Produced by Bookmart Limited
Desford Road, Enderby
Leicester LE9 5AD, England

ISBN 1-894102-16-9

Reprinted 1998

Printed in Italy

CONTENTS

ANIMALS AND BIRDS

The Owl and the Pussy-Cat 8
Jabberwocky 10
Hurt No Living Thing 12
Auguries of Innocence 12
How Doth the Little
    Crocodile 14
The Herring Loves the
    Merry Moonlight 15
The Maldive Shark 15
My Cat Jeoffry 16
The Owl 18
The Silver Swan 19
The Eagle 19
The Tyger 20

WEATHER AND SEASONS

Whether the Weather Be Fine 22
It's Raining, It's Pouring 22
The Rainbow 23
The Wind 24
The North Wind Doth Blow 24
Windy Nights 25

The Human Seasons 26
Winter 28
Spring 29
From Rain in Summer 30
Fall, Leaves, Fall 31
The Year's at the Spring 32

BRIGHT AND BEAUTIFUL

Pied Beauty 34
Daffodils 35
My Shadow 36
The Ecchoing Green 38
She Walks in Beauty 40
Shall I Compare Thee to a
    Summer's Day? 41
Blow, Bugle, Blow 42

DREAMS AND WONDERS

Kubla Khan	44
The Fairies	46
La Belle Dame Sans Merci	48
I Saw a Peacock	50
A Child's Thought	50

SONGS OF THE SEA

Full Fathom Five	52
What Are Heavy?	53
I Started Early	54
O Captain! My Captain!	56
Break, Break, Break	58
Meeting at Night	60

TALES OF TRAVEL

Ozymandias	62
Where Lies the Land?	63
Eldorado	64
Foreign Lands	66
Uphill	67
Travel	68
From a Railway Carriage	70

CHILDHOOD

Little Orphant Annie	72
Monday's Child	74
A Child's Grace	75
I Remember, I Remember	76
Swing, Swing	78
Good and Bad Children	80

AT THE END OF THE DAY

Escape at Bedtime	82
Bed in Summer	84
Is the Moon Tired?	85
Wynken, Blynken, and Nod	86
Star Light, Star Bright	88
How Many Miles to Babylon?	88
Hush Little Baby	89
Sleep, Baby, Sleep!	90

About the Poets	92
Index of Titles and First Lines	95

Animals and Birds

The Owl and the Pussy-Cat

The Owl and the Pussy-Cat went to sea
In a beautiful pea-green boat,
They took some honey, and plenty of money;
Wrapped up in a five-pound note.
The Owl looked up to the stars above,
And sang to a small guitar,
"O lovely Pussy, O Pussy, my love,
What a beautiful Pussy you are,
    You are,
    You are!
What a beautiful Pussy you are!"

Pussy said to the Owl, "You elegant fowl!
How charmingly sweet you sing!
O let us be married! too long we have tarried:
But what shall we do for a ring?"
They sailed away for a year and a day,
To the land where the Bong-tree grows,
And there in a wood a Piggy-wig stood,
With a ring at the end of his nose,
    His nose,
    His nose,
With a ring at the end of his nose.

"Dear Pig, are you willing to sell for one shilling
Your ring?" Said the Piggy, "I will."
So they took it away, and were married next day
By the Turkey who lives on the hill.
They dined on mince, and slices of quince,
Which they ate with a runcible spoon;
And hand in hand, on the edge of the sand,
They danced by the light of the moon,
    The moon,
    The moon,
They danced by the light of the moon.

Edward Lear

9

Jabberwocky

'Twas brillig, and the slithy toves
Did gyre and gimble in the wabe:
All mimsy were the borogoves,
And the mome raths outgrabe.

"Beware the Jabberwock, my son!
The jaws that bite, the claws that catch!
Beware the Jubjub bird, and shun
The frumious Bandersnatch!"

He took his vorpal sword in hand:
Long time the manxome foe he sought –
So rested he by the Tumtum tree,
And stood awhile in thought.

And, as in uffish thought he stood,
The Jabberwock, with eyes of flame,
Came whiffling through the tulgey wood,
And burbled as it came!

One, two! One, two! And through and through
The vorpal blade went snicker-snack!
He left it dead, and with its head
He went galumphing back.

"And hast thou slain the Jabberwock?
Come to my arms, my beamish boy!
O frabjous day! Callooh! Callay!"
He chortled in his joy.

'Twas brillig, and the slithy toves
Did gyre and gimble in the wabe:
All mimsy were the borogoves,
And the mome raths outgrabe.

Lewis Carroll

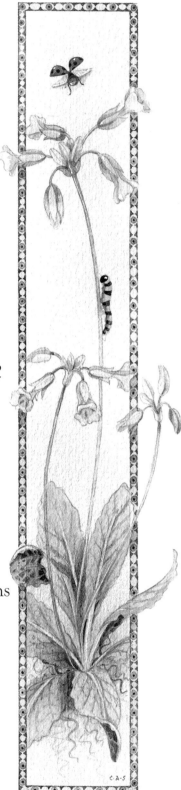

Hurt No Living Thing

Hurt no living thing;
Ladybird, nor butterfly,
Nor moth with dusty wing,
Nor cricket chirping cheerily,
Nor grasshopper so light of leap,
Nor dancing gnat, nor beetle fat,
Nor harmless worms that creep.

Christina Rossetti

Auguries of Innocence

To see a World in a Grain of Sand
And a Heaven in a Wild Flower,
Hold Infinity in the palm of your hand
And Eternity in an hour.

A Robin Red breast in a Cage
Puts all Heaven in a Rage.
A dove house fill'd with doves & Pigeons
Shudders Hell thro' all its regions.
A dog starv'd at his Master's Gate
Predicts the ruin of the State.
A Horse misus'd upon the Road
Calls to Heaven for Human blood.

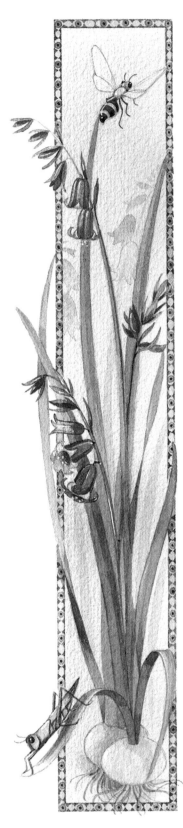

Each outcry of the hunted Hare
A fibre from the Brain does tear.
A Skylark wounded in the wing,
A Cherubim does cease to sing.
The Game Cock clip'd & arm'd for fight
Does the Rising Sun affright.
Every Wolf's & Lion's howl
Raises from Hell a Human Soul.
The wild deer, wand'ring here & there,
Keeps the Human Soul from Care.
The Lamb misus'd breeds Public strife
And yet forgives the Butcher's Knife.
The Bat that flits at close of Eve
Has left the Brain that won't Believe.
The Owl that calls upon the Night
Speaks the Unbeliever's fright.
He who shall hurt the little Wren
Shall never be belov'd by Men.
He who the Ox to wrath has mov'd
Shall never be by Woman lov'd.
The wanton Boy that kills the Fly
Shall fell the Spider's enmity.
He who torments the Chafer's sprite
Weaves a Bower in endless Night.
The Catterpiller on the Leaf
Repeats to thee thy Mother's grief.
Kill not the Moth nor Butterfly,
For the Last Judgment draweth nigh.

William Blake

13

How Doth the Little Crocodile

How doth the little crocodile
Improve his shining tail;
And pour the waters of the Nile
On every golden scale!

How cheerfully he seems to grin,
How neatly spreads his claws,
And welcomes little fishes in,
With gently smiling jaws!

Lewis Carroll

The Herring Loves the Merry Moonlight

The herring loves the merry moonlight,
The mackerel loves the wind,
But the oyster loves the dredging sang,
For they come of a gentle kind.

Sir Walter Scott

The Maldive Shark

About the Shark, phlegmatical one,
Pale sot of the Maldive sea,
The sleek little pilot-fish, azure and slim,
How alert in attendance be.
From his saw-pit of mouth, from his charnel of maw
They have nothing of harm to dread,
But liquidly glide on his ghastly flank
Or before his Gorgonian head;
Or luck in the port of serrated teeth
In white triple tiers of glittering gates,
And there find a haven when peril's abroad,
An asylum in jaws of the Fates!
They are friends; and friendly they guide him to prey,
Yet never partake of the treat –
Eyes and brains to the dotard lethargic and dull,
Pale ravener of horrible meat.

Herman Melville

My Cat Jeoffry

For I will consider my cat Jeoffry.
For he is the servant of the Living God,
 duly and daily serving him.
For at the first glance of the glory of God in
 the East he worships in his way.
For is this done by wreathing his body seven
 times round with elegant quickness.
For then he leaps up to catch the musk,
 which is the blessing of God upon his prayer.
For he rolls upon prank to work it in.
For having done duty and received blessing
 he begins to consider himself.
For this he performs in ten degrees.
For first he looks upon his fore-paws to see if
 they are clean.
For secondly he kicks up behind to clear away
 there.
For thirdly he works it upon stretch with the
 fore-paws extended.
For fourthly he sharpens his paws by wood.
For fifthly he washes himself.
For sixthly he rolls upon wash.
For seventhly he fleas himself, that he may not
 be interrupted upon the beat.
For eighthly he rubs himself against a post.
For ninthly he looks up for his instructions.
For tenthly he goes in quest of food.
For having considered God and himself he will
 consider his neighbour.

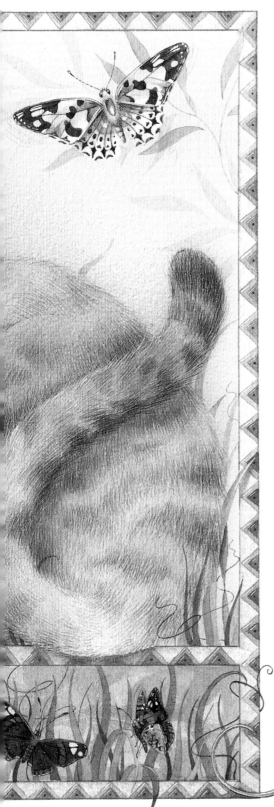

For if he meets another cat he will kiss her in
    kindness.
For when he takes his prey he plays with it to
    give it chance.
For one mouse in seven escapes by his
    dallying.
For when his day's work is done his business
    more properly begins.
For he keeps the Lord's watch in the night
    against the adversary.
For he counteracts the powers of darkness
    by his electrical skin & glaring eyes.
For he counteracts the Devil, who is death,
    by brisking about the life.
For in his morning orisons he loves the sun
    and the sun loves him.
For he is of the tribe of Tiger.
For the Cherub Cat is a term of the Angel Tiger.
For he has the subtlety and hissing of a serpent,
    which in goodness he suppresses.
For he will not do destruction, if he is well-fed,
    neither will he spit without provocation.
For he purrs in thankfulness, when God tells
    him he's a good Cat.
For he is an instrument for the children to learn
    benevolence upon.
For every house is incompleat without him &
    a blessing is lacking in the spirit.

Christopher Smart

The Owl

When cats run home and light is come,
And dew is cold upon the ground,
And the far-off stream is dumb,
And the whirring sail goes round,
And the whirring sail goes round;
Alone and warming his five wits,
The white owl in the belfry sits.

When merry milkmaids click the latch,
And rarely smells the new-mown hay,
And the cock hath sung beneath the thatch
Twice or thrice his roundelay,
Twice or thrice his roundelay;
Alone and warming his five wits,
The white owl in the belfry sits.

Alfred, Lord Tennyson

The Silver Swan

The silver swan, who living had no note,
When death approached, unlocked her silent throat,
Leaning her breast against the reedy shore,
Thus sung her first and last, and sung no more:
Farewell all joys! O death, come close mine eyes;
More geese than swans now live, more fools than wise.

Anonymous

The Eagle

He clasps the crag with crooked hands;
Close to the sun in lonely lands,
Ring'd with the azure world, he stands.

The wrinkled sea beneath him crawls;
He watches from his mountain walls,
And like a thunderbolt he falls.

Alfred, Lord Tennyson

The Tyger

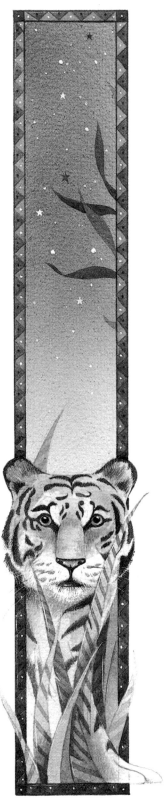

Tyger! Tyger! burning bright
In the forests of the night,
What immortal hand or eye
Could frame thy fearful symmetry?

In what distant deeps or skies
Burnt the fire of thine eyes?
On what wings dare he aspire?
What the hand dare seize the fire?

And what shoulder, & what art,
Could twist the sinews of thy heart?
And when thy heart began to beat,
What dread hand? & what dread feet?

What the hammer? what the chain?
In what furnace was thy brain?
What the anvil? what dread grasp
Dare its deadly terrors clasp?

When the stars threw down their spears,
And water'd heaven with their tears,
Did he smile his work to see?
Did he who made the Lamb make thee?

Tyger! Tyger! burning bright
In the forests of the night,
What immortal hand or eye,
Could frame thy fearful symmetry?

William Blake

WEATHER
and
SEASONS

Whether the Weather Be Fine

Whether the weather be fine
Or whether the weather be not,
Whether the weather be cold
Or whether the weather be hot,
We'll weather the weather
Whatever the weather,
Whether we like it or not.

Anonymous

It's Raining, It's Pouring

It's raining, it's pouring,
The old man is snoring;
He went to bed and bumped his head
And couldn't get up in the morning!

Anonymous

22

The Rainbow

Boats sail on the rivers,
And ships sail on the seas;
But clouds that sail across the sky
Are prettier far than these.

There are bridges on the rivers,
As pretty as you please;
But the bow that bridges heaven,
And overtops the trees,
And builds a road from earth to sky,
Is prettier far than these.

Christina Rossetti

The Wind

Who has seen the wind?
Neither I nor you;
But when the leaves hang trembling
The wind is passing through.

Who has seen the wind?
Neither you nor I;
But when the trees bow down their heads
The wind is passing by.

Christina Rossetti

The North Wind Doth Blow

The north wind doth blow,
And we shall have snow,
And what will poor robin do then,
Poor thing?

He'll sit in a barn,
And keep himself warm,
And hide his head under his wing,
Poor thing.

Anonymous

24

Windy Nights

Whenever the moon and stars are set,
　　Whenever the wind is high,
All night long in the dark and wet,
　　A man goes riding by.
Late in the night when the fires are out,
Why does he gallop and gallop about?

Whenever the trees are crying aloud,
　　And ships are tossed at sea,
By, on the highway, low and loud,
　　By at the gallop goes he.
By at the gallop he goes, and then
By he comes back at the gallop again.

Robert Louis Stevenson

The Human Seasons

Four seasons fill the measure of the year;
There are four seasons in the mind of man:
He has his lusty Spring, when fancy clear
Takes in all beauty with an easy span:

He has his Summer, when luxuriously
Spring's honey'd cud of youthful thought he loves
To ruminate, and by such dreaming nigh
His nearest unto heaven: quiet coves

His soul has in its Autumn, when his wings
He furleth close; contented so to look
On mists in idleness – to let fair things
Pass by unheeded as a threshold brook:

He has his Winter too of pale misfeature,
Or else he would forgo his mortal nature.

John Keats

Winter

When icicles hang by the wall,
And Dick the shepherd blows his nail,
And Tom bears logs into the hall,
And milk comes frozen home in pail;
When blood is nipped, and ways be foul,
Then nightly sings the staring owl.
Tu-whit, tu-who! a merry note,
While greasy Joan doth keel the pot.

When all aloud the wind doth blow,
And coughing drowns the parson's saw,
And birds sit brooding in the snow,
And Marian's nose looks red and raw,
When roasted crabs hiss in the bowl,
Then nightly sings the staring owl,
Tu-whit, tu-who! a merry note,
While greasy Joan doth keel the pot.

William Shakespeare

Spring

Sound the Flute!
Now it's mute.
Birds delight
Day and Night;
Nightingale
In the dale,
Lark in Sky,
Merrily,
Merrily, Merrily, to welcome in the Year.

Little Boy,
Full of joy;
Little Girl,
Sweet and small;
Cock does crow,
So do you;
Merry voice,
Infant noise,
Merrily, Merrily, to welcome in the Year.

Little Lamb,
Here I am;
Come and lick
My white neck;
Let me pull
Your soft Wool;
Let me kiss
Your soft face:
Merrily, Merrily, we welcome in the Year.

William Blake

From *Rain in Summer*

How beautiful is the rain!
After the dust and heat,
In the broad and fiery street,
In the narrow lane,
How beautiful is the rain!

How it clatters along the roofs,
Like the tramp of hoofs!
How it gushes and struggles out
From the throat of the overflowing spout!

Across the window-pane
It pours and pours;
And swift and wide,
With a muddy tide,
Like a river down the gutter roars
The rain, the welcome rain!

Henry Wadsworth Longfellow

Fall, Leaves, Fall

Fall, leaves, fall: die, flowers, away;
Lengthen night and shorten day,
Every leaf speaks bliss to me
Fluttering from the autumn tree.
I shall smile when wreaths of snow
Blossom where the rose should grow;
I shall sing when night's decay
Ushers in a drearier day.

Emily Brontë

The Year's at the Spring

The year's at the spring
And day's at the morn;
Morning's at seven;
The hill-side's dew-pearled;
The lark's on the wing;
The snail's on the thorn:
God's in his heaven –
All's right with the world!

Robert Browning

 BRIGHT and BEAUTIFUL

Pied Beauty

Glory be to God for dappled things –
For skies of couple-colour as a brinded cow;
For rose-moles all in stipple upon trout that swim;
Fresh-firecoal chestnut-falls; finches' wings;
Landscape plotted and pieced – fold, fallow, and plough;
And all trades, their gear and tackle and trim.

All things counter, original, spare, strange;
Whatever is fickle, freckled (who knows how?)
With swift, slow; sweet, sour; adazzle, dim;
He fathers-forth whose beauty is past change:
                                        Praise him

Gerard Manley Hopkins

Daffodils

I wandered lonely as a cloud
    That floats on high o'er vales and hills,
When all at once I saw a crowd,
    A host, of golden daffodils;
Beside the lake, beneath the trees,
Fluttering and dancing in the breeze.

Continuous as the stars that shine
    And twinkle on the Milky Way,
They stretched in never-ending line
    Along the margin of a bay:
Ten thousand saw I at a glance,
Tossing their heads in sprightly dance.

The waves beside them danced, but they
    Out-did the sparkling waves in glee:
A poet could not but be gay,
    In such a jocund company:
I gazed – and gazed – but little thought
What wealth the show to me had brought:

For oft, when on my couch I lie
    In vacant or in pensive mood,
They flash upon that inward eye
    Which is the bliss of solitude;
And then my heart with pleasure fills,
And dances with the daffodils.

William Wordsworth

My Shadow

I have a little shadow that goes in and out with me,
And what can be the use of him is more than I can see.
He is very, very like me from the heels up to the head;
And I see him jump before me, when I jump into my bed.

The funniest thing about him is the way he likes to grow –
Not at all like proper children, which is always very slow;
For he sometimes shoots up taller like an india-rubber ball,
And he sometimes gets so little that there's none of him at all.

He hasn't got a notion of how children ought to play,
And can only make a fool of me in every sort of way.
He stays so close behind me he's a coward you can see;
I'd think shame to stick to nursie as that shadow sticks to me!

One morning, very early, before the sun was up,
I rose and found the shining dew on every buttercup;
But my lazy little shadow, like an arrant sleepy-head,
Had stayed at home behind me and was fast asleep in bed.

Robert Louis Stevenson

The Ecchoing Green

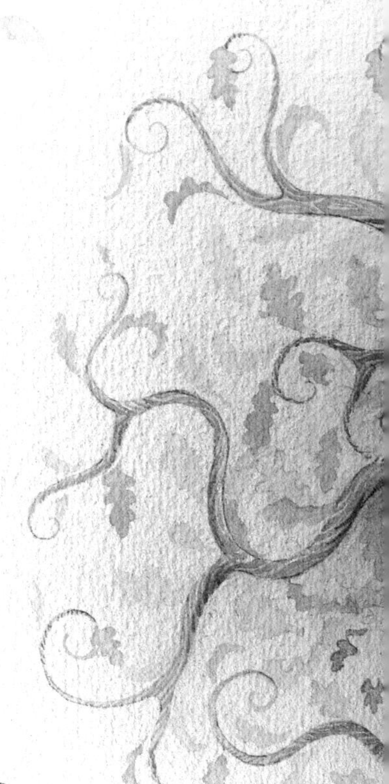

The sun does arise;
And make happy the skies.
The merry bells ring
To welcome the Spring;
The skylark and thrush,
The birds of the bush,
Sing louder around
To the bells' chearful sound,
While our sports shall be seen
On the Ecchoing Green.

Old John, with white hair,
Does laugh away care,
Sitting under the oak,
Among the old folk.
They laugh at our play,
And soon they all say:
"Such, such were the joys
When we all, girls & boys,
In our youth time were seen
On the Ecchoing Green."

Till the little ones, weary,
No more can be merry;
The sun does descend,
And our sports have an end.
Round the laps of their mothers
Many sisters and brothers,
Like birds in their nest,
Are ready for rest,
And sport no more seen
On the darkening Green.

William Blake

She Walks in Beauty

She walks in beauty, like the night
    Of cloudless climes and starry skies;
And all that's best of dark and bright
    Meet in her aspect and her eyes:
Thus mellowed to that tender light
    Which heaven to gaudy day denies.

One shade the more, one ray the less,
    Had half impaired the nameless grace
Which waves in every raven tress,
    Or softly lightens o'er her face;
Where thoughts serenely sweet express
    How pure, how dear their dwelling-place.

And on that cheek, and o'er that brow,
    So soft, so calm, yet eloquent,
The smiles that win, the tints that glow,
    But tell of days in goodness spent,
A mind at peace with all below,
    A heart whose love is innocent.

George Gordon, Lord Byron

Shall I Compare Thee to a Summer's Day?

Shall I compare thee to a summer's day?
  Thou art more lovely and more temperate:
Rough winds do shake the darling buds of May,
  And summer's lease hath all too short a date:
Sometime too hot the eye of heaven shines,
  And often is his gold complexion dimmed;
And every fair from fair sometime declines,
  By chance, or nature's changing course untrimmed;
But thy eternal summer shall not fade,
  Nor lose possession of that fair thou owest,
Nor shall Death brag thou wanderest in his shade,
  When in eternal lines to time thou growest;
So long as men can breathe, or eyes can see,
So long lives this, and this gives life to thee.

William Shakespeare

41

Blow, Bugle, Blow

The splendour falls on castle walls
    And snowy summits old in story:
The long light shakes across the lakes,
    And the wild cataract leaps in glory.
Blow, bugle, blow, set the wild echoes flying,
Blow, bugle; answer, echoes, dying, dying, dying.

O hark, O hear! how thin and clear,
    And thinner, clearer, farther going!
O sweet and far from cliff and scar
    The horns of Elfland faintly blowing!
Blow, let us hear the purple glens replying:
Blow, bugle; answer, echoes, dying, dying, dying.

O love, they die in yon rich sky,
    They faint on hill or field or river:
Our echoes roll from soul to soul,
    And grow for ever and for ever.
Blow, bugle, blow, set the wild echoes flying,
And answer, echoes, answer, dying, dying, dying.

Alfred, Lord Tennyson

DREAMS
and
WONDERS

Kubla Khan

In Xanadu did Kubla Khan
    A stately pleasure-dome decree:
Where Alph, the sacred river, ran
Through caverns measureless to man
    Down to a sunless sea.
So twice five miles of fertile ground
    With walls and towers were girdled round:
And there were gardens bright with sinuous rills
Where blossomed many an incense-bearing tree;
And here were forests ancient as the hills,
Enfolding sunny spots of greenery.

But O, that deep romantic chasm which slanted
Down the green hill athwart a cedarn cover!
A savage place! as holy and enchanted
As e'er beneath a waning moon was haunted
By woman wailing for her demon-lover!
And from this chasm, with ceaseless turmoil seething,
As if this earth in fast thick pants were breathing,
A mighty fountain momently was forced;
Amid whose swift half-intermitted burst
Huge fragments vaulted like rebounding hail,
Or chaffy grain beneath the thresher's flail:
And 'mid these dancing rocks at once and ever
It flung up momently the sacred river.
Five miles meandering with a mazy motion
Through wood and dale the sacred river ran,
Then reached the caverns measureless to man,
And sank in tumult to a lifeless ocean:
And 'mid this tumult Kubla heard from far
Ancestral voices prophesying war!

44

The shadow of the dome of pleasure
  Floated midway on the waves;
Where was heard the mingled measure
  From the fountain and the caves.
It was a miracle of rare device,
A sunny pleasure-dome with caves of ice!

A damsel with a dulcimer
  In a vision once I saw:
It was an Abyssinian maid,
  And on her dulcimer she played,
Singing of Mount Abora.
Could I revive within me,
  Her symphony and song,
To such a deep delight 'twould win me,
That with music loud and long,
I would build that dome in air,
That sunny dome! those caves of ice!
And all who heard should see them there,
And all should cry, Beware! Beware!
His flashing eyes, his floating hair!
  Weave a circle round him thrice,
   And close your eyes with holy dread,
For he on honey-dew hath fed,
  And drunk the milk of Paradise.

Samuel Taylor Coleridge

The Fairies

Up the airy mountain,
Down the rushy glen,
We daren't go a-hunting
For fear of little men;
Wee folk, good folk,
Trooping all together;
Green jacket, red cap,
And white owl's feather!

Down along the rocky shore
Some make their home,
They live on crispy pancakes
Of yellow tide-foam;
Some in the reeds
Of the black mountain lake,
With frogs for their watch-dogs,
All night awake.

High on the hill-top
The old King sits;
He is now so old and gray
He's right lost his wits.
With a bridge of white mist
Columbkill he crosses,
On his stately journeys
From Slieveleague to Rosses;
Or going up with music
On cold starry nights
To sup with the Queen
Of the gay Northern Lights.

They stole little Bridget
For seven years long;
When she came down again
Her friends were all gone.
They took her lightly back,
Between the night and morrow,
They thought that she was fast asleep,
But she was dead with sorrow.
They have kept her ever since
Deep within the lake,
On a bed of flag-leaves,
Watching till she wake.

By the craggy hill-side,
Through the mosses bare,
They have planted thorn-trees
For pleasure here and there.
Is any man so daring
As dig them up in spite,
He shall find their sharpest thorns
In his bed at night.

Up the airy mountain,
Down the rushy glen,
We daren't go a-hunting
For fear of little men;
Wee folk, good folk,
Trooping all together;
Green jacket, red cap,
And white owl's feather!

William Allingham

La Belle Dame Sans Merci

O what can ail thee, knight-at-arms,
Alone and palely loitering?
The sedge has wither'd from the lake,
And no birds sing.

O what can ail thee, knight-at-arms,
So haggard and so woe-begone?
The squirrel's granary is full,
And the harvest's done.

I see a lily on thy brow,
With anguish moist and fever dew;
And on thy cheeks a fading rose
Fast withereth too.

I met a lady in the meads,
Full beautiful – a faery's child,
Her hair was long, her foot was light,
And her eyes were wild.

I made a garland for her head,
And bracelets too, and fragrant zone;
She look'd at me as she did love,
And made sweet moan.

I set her on my pacing steed,
And nothing else saw all day long;
For sidelong would she bend, and sing
A faery's song.

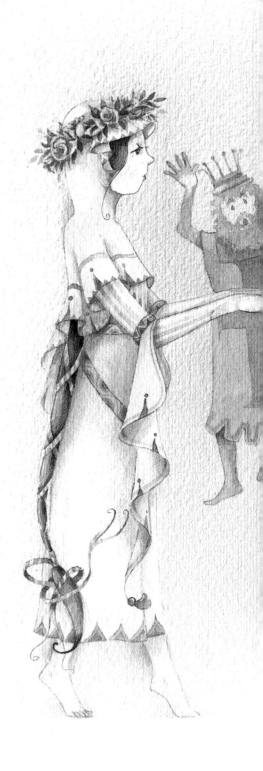

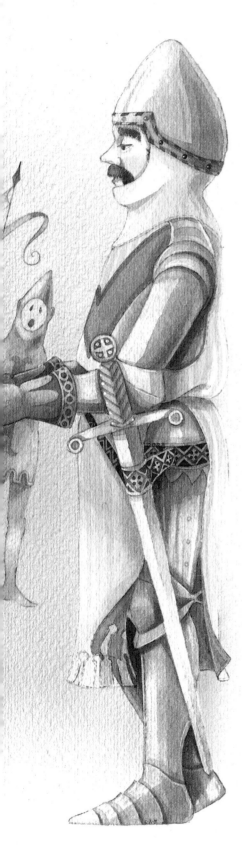

She found me roots of relish sweet,
And honey wild, and manna dew,
And sure in language strange she said –
"I love thee true".

She took me to her elfin grot,
And there she wept and sigh'd full sore,
And there I shut her wild wild eyes
With kisses four.

And there she lulled me asleep
And there I dream'd – Ah! woe betide!
The latest dream I ever dream'd
On the cold hill side.

I saw pale kings and princes too,
Pale warriors, death-pale were they all;
They cried – "La Belle Dame sans Merci
Hath thee in thrall!"

I saw their starved lips in the gloam,
With horrid warning gaped wide,
And I awoke and found me here,
On the cold hill's side.

And this is why I sojourn here
Alone and palely loitering,
Though the sedge has wither'd from the lake,
And no birds sing.

John Keats

I Saw a Peacock

I saw a peacock with a fiery tail
I saw a blazing comet drop down hail
I saw a cloud wrapped with ivy round
I saw an oak creep upon the ground
I saw a pismire swallow up a whale
I saw the sea brimful of ale
I saw a Venice glass full fifteen feet deep
I saw a well full of men's tears that weep
I saw red eyes all of a flaming fire
I saw a house bigger than the moon and higher
I saw the sun at twelve o'clock at night
I saw the man that saw this wondrous sight.

Anonymous

A Child's Thought

At seven, when I go to bed,
I find such pictures in my head:
Castles with dragons prowling round,
Gardens where magic fruits are found;
Fair ladies prisoned in a tower,
Or lost in an enchanted bower;
While gallant horsemen ride by streams
That border all this land of dreams
I find, so clearly in my head
At seven, when I go to bed.

Robert Louis Stevenson

Songs
of
The Sea

Full Fathom Five

Full fathom five they father lies;
    Of his bones are coral made;
Those are pearls that were his eyes:
    Nothing of him that doth fade,
But doth suffer a sea-change
Into something rich and strange:
Sea nymphs hourly ring his knell.
            Ding-dong!
Hark! now I hear them,
          Ding-dong, bell!

William Shakespeare

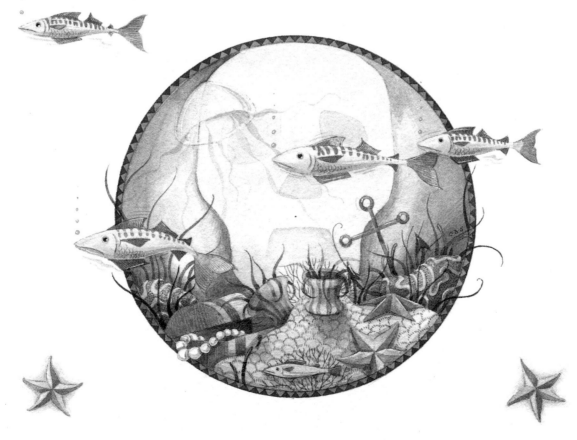

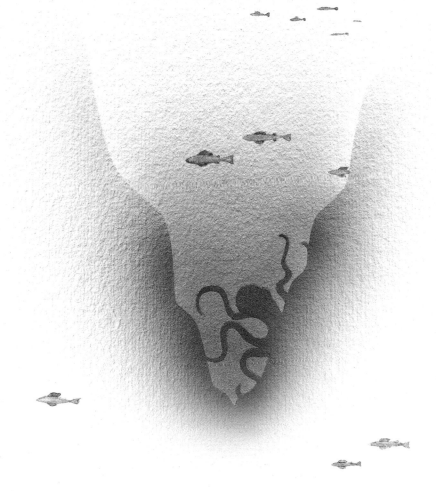

What Are Heavy?

What are heavy? sea-sand and sorrow:
What are brief? today and tomorrow:
What are frail? Spring blossoms and youth:
What are deep? the ocean and truth.

Christina Rossetti

I Started Early

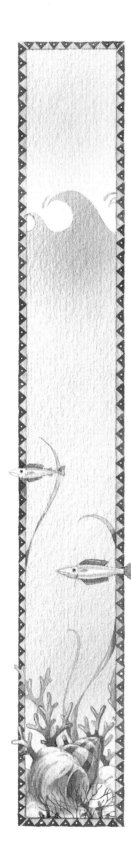

I started Early – Took my Dog –
And visited the Sea –
The Mermaids in the Basement
Came out to look at me –

And Frigates – in the Upper Floor
Extended Hempen Hands –
Presuming Me to be a Mouse –
Aground – upon the Sands –

But no Man moved Me – till the Tide
Went past my simple Shoe –
And past my Apron – and my Belt
And past my Bodice – too –

And made as He would eat me up –
As wholly as a Dew
Upon a Dandelion's Sleeve –
And then – I started – too –

And He – He followed – close behind –
I felt His Silver Heel
Upon my Ankle – Then my Shoes
Would overflow with Pearl –

Until We met the Solid Town –
No One He seemed to know –
And bowing – with a Mighty look –
At me – The Sea withdrew –

Emily Dickinson

O Captain! My Captain!

O Captain! my Captain! our fearful trip is done,
The ship has weather'd every rack, the prize we sought is won,
The port is near, the bells I hear, the people all exulting,
While follow eyes the steady keel, the vessel grim and daring;
    But O heart! heart! heart!
    O the bleeding drops of red,
      Where on the deck my Captain lies,
      Fallen cold and dead.

O Captain! my Captain! rise up and hear the bells;
Rise up – for you the flag is flung – for you the bugle trills,
For you bouquets and ribbon'd wreaths – for you the shores a-crowding,
For you they call, the swaying mass, their eager faces turning;
    Here Captain! dear father!
    This arm beneath your head!
    It is some dream that on the deck,
    You've fallen cold and dead.

My Captain does not answer, his lips are pale and still,
My father does not feel my arm, he has no pulse nor will,
The ship is anchor'd safe and sound, its voyage closed and done,
From fearful trip the victor ship comes in with object won;
    Exult O shores, and ring O bells!
    But I with mournful tread,
    Walk the deck my Captain lies,
    Fallen cold and dead.

Walt Whitman

Break, Break, Break

Break, break, break,
    On thy cold gray stones, O Sea!
And I would that my tongue could utter
    The thoughts that arise in me.

O well for the fisherman's boy,
    That he shouts with his sister at play!
O well for the sailor lad,
    That he sings in his boat on the bay!

And the stately ships go on
    To their haven under the hill;
But O for the touch of a vanish'd hand,
    And the sound of a voice that is still!

Break, break, break,
    At the foot of thy crags, O sea!
But the tender grace of a day that is dead
    Will never come back to me.

Alfred, Lord Tennyson

Meeting at Night

The gray sea and the long black land;
And the yellow half-moon large and low;
And the startled little waves that leap
In fiery ringlets from their sleep,
As I gain the cove with pushing prow,
And quench its speed i' the slushy sand.

Then a mile of warm sea-scented beach;
Three fields to cross till a farm appears;
A tap at the pane, the quick sharp scratch
And blue spurt of a lighted match,
And a voice less loud, thro' its joys and fears,
Than the two hearts beating each to each!

Robert Browning

TALES
of
TRAVEL

Ozymandias

I met a traveller from an antique land
Who said: Two vast and trunkless legs of stone
Stand in the desert ... Near them, on the sand,
Half sunk, a shattered visage lies, whose frown,
And wrinkled lip, and sneer of cold command,
Tell that its sculptor well those passions read
Which yet survive, stamped on these lifeless things,
The hand that mocked them, and the heart that fed:
And on the pedestal these words appear:
"My name is Ozymandias, king of kings:
Look on my works, ye Mighty, and despair!"
Nothing beside remains. Round the decay
Of that colossal wreck, boundless and bare
The lone and level sands stretch far away.

Percy Bysshe Shelley

Where Lies the Land?

Where lies the land to which the ship would go?
Far, far ahead, is all her seamen know.
And where the land she travels from? Away,
Far, far behind, is all that they can say.

On sunny noons upon the deck's smooth face,
Linked arm in arm, how pleasant here to pace;
Or, o'er the stern reclining, watch below
The foaming wake far widening as we go.

On stormy nights when wild north-westers rave,
How proud a thing to fight with wind and wave!
The dripping sailor on the reeling mast
Exults to bear, and scorns to wish it past.

Where lies the land to which the ship would go?
Far, far ahead, is all her seamen know.
And where the land she travels from? Away,
Far, far behind, is all that they can say.

Arthur Hugh Clough

Eldorado

Gaily bedight,
A gallant knight,
In sunshine and in shadow,
Had journeyed long,
Singing a song,
In search of Eldorado.

But he grew old –
This knight so bold –
And o'er his heart a shadow
Fell, as he found
No spot of ground
That looked like Eldorado.

And, as his strength
Failed him at length,
He met a pilgrim shadow –
"Shadow," said he,
"Where can it be –
This land of Eldorado?"

"Over the Mountains
Of the Moon,
Down the Valley of the Shadow,
Ride, boldly ride,"
The shade replied,
"If you seek for Eldorado!"

Edgar Allan Poe

65

Foreign Lands

Up into the cherry-tree
Who should climb but little me?
I held the trunk with both my hands
And looked abroad on foreign lands.

I saw the next-door garden lie,
Adorned with flowers before my eye,
And many pleasant places more
That I had never seen before.

I saw the dimpling river pass
And be the sky's blue looking-glass;
The dusty roads go up and down
With people tramping in to town.

If I could find a higher tree
Farther and farther I should see,
To where the grown-up river slips
Into the sea among the ships,

To where the roads on either hand
Lead onward into fairy land,
Where all the children dine at five,
And all the playthings come alive.

Robert Louis Stevenson

Uphill

Does the road wind uphill all the way?
Yes, to the very end.
Will the day's journey take the whole long day?
From morn to night, my friend.

But is there for the night a resting-place?
A roof for when the slow, dark hours begin.
May not the darkness hide it from my face?
You cannot miss that inn.

Shall I meet other wayfarers at night?
Those who have gone before.
Then must I knock, or call when just in sight?
They will not keep you waiting at that door.

Shall I find comfort, travel-sore and weak?
Of labour you shall find the sum.
Will there be beds for me and all who seek?
Yea, beds for all who come.

Christina Rossetti

Travel

I should like to rise and go
Where the golden apples grow;
Where below another sky
Parrot islands anchored lie,
And, watched by cockatoos and goats,
Lonely Crusoes building boats;
Where in sunshine reaching out
Eastern cities, miles about,
Are with mosque and minaret
Among sandy gardens set,
And the rich goods from near and far
Hang for sale in the bazaar;
Where the Great Wall round China goes,
And on one side the desert blows,
And with bell and voice and drum,
Cities on the other hum;

Where are forests, hot as fire,
Wide as England, tall as a spire,
Full of apes and coco-nuts
And the negro hunters' huts;
Where the knotty crocodile
Lies and blinks in the Nile,
And the red flamingo flies
Hunting fish before his eyes;

Where in jungles, near and far,
Man-devouring tigers are,
Lying close and giving ear
Lest the hunt be drawing near,
Or a comer-by be seen
Swinging in a palanquin;
Where among the desert sands
Some deserted city stands,

All its children, sweep and prince,
Grown to manhood ages since,
Not a foot in street or house,
Not a stir of child or mouse,
And when kindly falls the night,
In all the town no spark of light.
There I'll come when I'm a man
With a camel caravan;
Light a fire in the gloom
Of some dusty dining-room;
See the pictures on the walls,
Heroes, fights and festivals;
And in a corner find the toys
Of the old Egyptian boys.

Robert Louis Stevenson

From a Railway Carriage

Faster than fairies, faster than witches,
Bridges and houses, hedges and ditches;
And charging along like troops in a battle,
All through the meadows the horses and cattle:
All of the sights of the hill and the plain
Fly as thick as driving rain;
And ever again, in the wink of an eye,
Painted stations whistle by.

Here is a child who clambers and scrambles,
All by himself and gathering brambles;
Here is a tramp who stands and gazes;
And there is the green for stringing the daisies!
Here is a cart run away in the road
Lumping along with man and load;
And here is a mill, and there is a river:
Each a glimpse and gone for ever!

Robert Louis Stevenson

CHILDHOOD

Little Orphant Annie

Little Orphant Annie's come to our house to stay,
An' wash the cups and saucers up, an' brush the crumbs away,
An' shoo the chickens off the porch, an' dust the hearth, an' sweep,
An' make the fire, an' bake the bread, an' earn her board-an'-keep;
An' all us other children, when the supper things is done,
We set around the kitchen fire an' has the mostest fun
A-list'nin' to the witch-tales 'at Annie tells about,
An' the Gobble-uns 'at gits you

    Ef you

        Don't

            Watch

                Out!

Wunst they was a little boy wouldn't say his prayers,–
An' when he went to bed at night, away up-stairs,
His Mammy heerd him holler, an' his Daddy heerd him bawl,
An' when they turn't the kivvers down, he wazn't there at all!
An' they seeked him in the rafter-room, an' cubby-hole, an' press,
An' seeked him up the chimbly-flue, an' ever'wheres, I guess;
But all they ever found wuz thist his pants an' round-about: –
An' the Gobble-uns 'll git you

    Ef you

        Don't

            Watch

                Out!

An' one time a little girl 'ud allus laugh and grin,
An' make fun of ever'one, an' all her blood-an'-kin;
An' wunst, when they wuz "company," an' ole folks wuz there,
She mocked 'em an' shocked 'em, an' said she didn't care!
An' thist as she kicked her heels, an' turn't to run an' hide,
They wuz two great big Black Things a-standin' by her side,
An' they snatched her through the ceilin' 'fore she knowed what she's
    about!
An' the Gobble-uns 'll git you
    Ef you
        Don't
           Watch
             Out!

An' little Orphant Annie says, when the blaze is blue,
An' the lamp wick sputters, an' the wind goes *woo-oo!*
An' you hear the crickets quit, an' the moon is gray,
An' the lightnin'-bugs in dew is all squenched away, –
You better mind yer parunts, an' yer teachers fond an' dear,
An' churish them 'at loves you, an' dry the orphant's tear,
An' he'p the pore an' needy ones 'at clusters all about,
Er the Gobble-uns 'll git you
    Ef you
        Don't
           Watch
             Out!

James Whitcomb Riley

73

Monday's Child

Monday's child is fair of face,
Tuesday's child is full of grace,
Wednesday's child is full of woe,
Thursday's child has far to go,
Friday's child is loving and giving,
Saturday's child works hard for his living,
And the child that is born on the Sabbath day
Is bonny and blithe, and good and gay.

Anonymous

A Child's Grace

Here a little child I stand
Heaving up my either hand;
Cold as paddocks though they be,
Here I lift them up to Thee,
For a benison to fall
On our meat and on us all.
                    Amen.

Robert Herrick

I Remember, I Remember

I remember, I remember,
The house where I was born,
The little window where the sun
Came peeping in at morn;
He never came a wink too soon,
Nor brought too long a day,
But now, I often wish the night
Had borne my breath away!

I remember, I remember,
The roses, red and white,
The violets, and the lily-cups,
Those flowers made of light!
The lilacs where the robin built,
And where my brother set
The laburnum on his birthday, –
The tree is living yet!

I remember, I remember,
Where I was used to swing,
And thought the air must rush as fresh
To swallows on the wing;
My spirit flew in feathers then,
That is so heavy now,
And summer pools could hardly cool
The fever on my brow!

I remember, I remember,
The fir trees dark and high;
I used to think their slender tops
Were close against the sky:
It was a childish ignorance,
But now 'tis little joy
To know I'm farther off from Heav'n
Than when I was a boy.

Thomas Hood

Swing, Swing

Swing, swing,
Sing, sing,
Here! my throne and I am a king!
Swing, swing,
Sing, sing,
Farewell, earth, for I'm on the wing!

Low, high,
Here I fly,
Like a bird through sunny sky;
Free, free,
Over the lea,
Over the mountain, over the sea!

Soon, soon,
Afternoon,
Over the sunset, over the moon;
Far, far,
Over all bar,
Sweeping on from star to star!

No, no,
Low, low,
Sweeping daisies with my toe.
Slow, slow,
To and fro,
Slow – slow – slow – slow.

William Allingham

Good and Bad Children

Children, you are very little,
And your bones are very brittle;
If you would grow great and stately,
You must try to walk sedately.

You must still be bright and quiet,
And content with simple diet;
And remain, through all bewild'ring.
Innocent and honest children.

Happy hearts and happy faces,
Happy play in grassy places –
That was how, in ancient ages,
Children grew to kings and sages.

But the unkind and the unruly,
And the sort to eat unduly,
They must never hope for glory –
Theirs is quite a different story!

Cruel children, crying babies,
All grow up as geese and gabies,
Hated, as their age increases,
By their nephews and their nieces.

Robert Louis Stevenson

80

AT THE END
of
THE DAY

Escape at Bedtime

The lights from the parlour and kitchen shone out
    Through the blinds and the windows and bars;
And high overhead and all moving about,
    There were thousands of millions of stars.
There ne'er were such thousands of leaves on a tree,
    Nor of people in church or the Park,
As the crowds of the stars looked down upon me,
    And that glittered and winked in the dark.

The Dog, and the Plough, and the Hunter, and all,
    And the star of the sailor, and Mars,
These shone in the sky, and the pail by the wall
    Would be half full of water and stars.
They saw me at last, and they chased me with cries,
    And they soon had me packed into bed;
But the glory kept shining and bright in my eyes,
    And the stars going round in my head.

Robert Louis Stevenson

82

83

Bed in Summer

In winter I get up at night
And dress by yellow candle-light.
In summer, quite the other way,
I have to go to bed by day.

I have to go to bed and see
The birds still hopping on the tree,
Or hear the grown-up people's feet
Still going past me in the street.

And does it not seem hard to you,
When all the sky is clear and blue,
And I should like so much to play,
To have to go to bed by day?

Robert Louis Stevenson

Is the Moon Tired?

Is the moon tired? She looks so pale
    Within her misty veil;
She scales the sky from east to west,
    And takes no rest.

Before the coming of the night
    The moon shows papery white;
Before the dawning of the day
    She fades away.

Christina Rossetti

Wynken, Blynken, and Nod

Wynken, Blynken, and Nod one night
Sailed off in a wooden shoe –
Sailed on a river of crystal light,
Into a sea of dew.
"Where are you going, and what do you wish?"
The old moon asked the three.
"We have come to fish for the herring fish
That live in this beautiful sea;
Nets of silver and gold have we!"
    Said Wynken,
    Blynken,
    And Nod.

The old moon laughed and sang a song
As they rocked in the wooden shoe,
And the wind that sped them all night long
Ruffled the waves of dew.
The little stars were the herring fish
That lived in that beautiful sea –
"Now cast your nets wherever you wish –
Never afeard are we";
So cried the stars to the fishermen three:
    Wynken,
    Blynken,
    And Nod.

All night long their nets they threw
To the stars in the twinkling foam –
Then down from the skies came the wooden shoe,
Bringing the fishermen home;
'Twas all so pretty a sail it seemed
As if it could not be,
And some folks thought 'twas a dream they'd dreamed
Of sailing that beautiful sea –
But I shall name you the fishermen three:
    Wynken,
    Blynken,
    And Nod.

Wynken and Blynken are two little eyes,
And Nod is a little head,
And the wooden shoe that sailed the skies
Is a wee one's trundle-bed.
So shut your eyes while mother sings
Of wonderful sights that be,
And you shall see the beautiful things
As you rock in the misty sea,
Where the old shoe rocked the fishermen three:
    Wynken,
    Blynken,
    And Nod.

Eugene Field

Star Light, Star Bright

Star light, star bright,
First star I see tonight,
I wish I may, I wish I might,
Have the wish I wish tonight.

Anonymous

How Many Miles to Babylon?

How many miles to Babylon?
    Three score miles and ten.
Can I get there by candlelight?
    Yes, and back again.
    If your heels are nimble and light,
    You may get there by candlelight.

Anonymous

Hush Little Baby

Hush little baby, don't say a word,
Papa's going to buy you a mockingbird.

If that mockingbird won't sing,
Papa's going to buy you a diamond ring.

If that diamond ring turns brass,
Papa's going to buy you a looking glass.

If that looking glass gets broke,
Papa's going to buy you a billy goat.

If that billy goat won't pull,
Papa's going to buy you a cart and bull.

If that cart and bull fall down,
You'll still be the sweetest little baby in town.

Anonymous

Sleep, Baby, Sleep!

Sleep, baby, sleep!
Your father herds his sheep:
Your mother shakes the little tree
From which fall pretty dreams on thee;
Sleep, baby, sleep!

Sleep, baby, sleep!
The heavens are white with sheep:
For they are lambs – those stars so bright:
And the moon's shepherd of the night;
Sleep, baby, sleep!

Sleep, baby, sleep!
And I'll give thee a sheep,
Which, with its golden bell, shall be
A little play-fellow for thee;
Sleep, baby, sleep!

Sleep, baby, sleep!
And bleat not like a sheep,
Or else the shepherd's angry dog
Will come and bite my naughty rogue;
Sleep, baby, sleep!

Sleep, baby, sleep!
Go out and herd the sheep,
Go out, you barking black dog, go,
And waken not my baby so;
Sleep, baby, sleep!

Anonymous

ABOUT THE POETS

WILLIAM ALLINGHAM
1824–89

Pages 46, 78 This Irish poet wrote many volumes of poetry, including some based on traditional Irish myths and legends.

WILLIAM BLAKE
1757–1827

Pages 12, 20, 29, 38 Born in London, Blake was a painter and engraver as well as a poet. He illustrated many of his own poems with vivid engravings.

EMILY BRONTE
1818–48

Page 31 One of the three famous Brontë sisters, Emily is best known for her only novel, *Wuthering Heights*, which she published under the name of Ellis Bell.

ROBERT BROWNING
1812–89

Pages 32, 60 Browning's poems attracted much attention during his lifetime, including that of fellow poet Elizabeth Barrett. They were married in 1846.

GEORGE GORDON, LORD BYRON
1788–1824

Page 40 A romantic figure, very popular during his lifetime, Byron died of fever in Greece, supporting a Greek uprising.

LEWIS CARROLL
1832–98

Pages 10, 14 Lewis Carroll's real name was Charles Dodgson. He was a mathematics lecturer in Oxford, England, but became famous for his children's books, *Alice's Adventures in Wonderland* and *Through the Looking Glass*, which are still read today.

ARTHUR HUGH CLOUGH
1819–61

Page 63 Clough's father emigrated to the U.S.A. His son returned to England to live and work, but had many American friends.

SAMUEL TAYLOR COLERIDGE
1772–1834

Page 44 A poet and thinker, Coleridge was a great friend of the poet William Wordsworth.

EMILY DICKINSON
1830–86
Page 54 This American poet lived a secluded life in Massachussets, writing over a thousand poems. Their original forms and use of language have influenced many modern poets.

EUGENE FIELD
1850–95
Page 86 This American journalist is now most famous for his poems for children.

ROBERT HERRICK
1591–1674
Page 75 This English poet wrote chiefly of love, youth and figures from ancient Greece and Rome.

 THOMAS HOOD
1799–1845
Page 76 Born in London, this poet and humorist contributed to many popular magazines.

GERARD MANLEY HOPKINS
1844–89
Page 34 As a young man, Hopkins became a Roman Catholic; many of his poems have a religious theme.

JOHN KEATS
1795–1821
Pages 26, 48 Trained as a doctor, Keats wrote many wonderful poems before dying, still a very young man, in Rome, Italy.

 EDWARD LEAR
1812–88
Page 8 An artist and author, Lear wrote many serious books but is best known for his *Book of Nonsense*, published in 1846.

HENRY WADSWORTH LONGFELLOW
1807–82
Page 30 As well as short poems, Longfellow enjoyed telling long stories in verse, such as *Hiawatha*.

HERMAN MELVILLE
1819–91
Page 15 Born in New York, Melville is perhaps most famous for his sea-faring novel, *Moby Dick*.

EDGAR ALLAN POE
1809–49
Page 64 This American poet and story-teller particularly enjoyed mysterious and spine-chilling subjects.

93

JAMES WHITCOMB RILEY
1849–1916
Page 72 This American poet was born in Indiana. "Little Orfant Annie" is his most famous poem.

CHRISTINA ROSSETTI
1830–94
Pages 12, 23, 24, 53, 67, 85 The poet's Italian father settled in London before her birth. She also had a famous brother, the painter and poet Dante Gabriel Rossetti.

SIR WALTER SCOTT
1771–1832
Page 15 A poet and novelist, Scott celebrated all things Scottish in his work.

WILLIAM SHAKESPEARE
1564–1616
Pages 28, 41, 52 Perhaps the greatest playwright in the English language, Shakespeare lived in England in the time of Elizabeth I.

PERCY BYSSHE SHELLEY
1792–1822
Page 62 Shelley shocked English society with his beliefs. His later years were spent abroad.

CHRISTOPHER SMART
1722–71
Page 16 As well as writing poetry, Smart also made translations of the Bible.

ROBERT LOUIS STEVENSON
1850–94
Pages 25, 36, 50, 66, 68, 70, 80, 82, 84 A popular writer of adventure stories, Stevenson is perhaps best known for his *Treasure Island.*

ALFRED, LORD TENNYSON
1809–92
Pages 18, 19, 42, 58 Tennyson's poems and verse-stories enjoyed huge popularity in his lifetime.

WALT WHITMAN
1819–92
Page 56 Whitman's varied life and experiences in the American Civil War are reflected in his poetry, but he did not find real fame until after his death.

WILLIAM WORDSWORTH
1770–1850
Page 35 Wordsworth is best known as a poet of nature, expressing his love for the Lake District, England.

INDEX OF TITLES AND FIRST LINES

About the Shark, phlegmatical one — 15

A Child's Grace — 75

A Child's Thought — 50

At seven, when I go to bed — 50

Auguries of Innocence — 12

Bed in Summer — 84

Blow, Bugle, Blow — 42

Boats sail on the rivers — 23

Break, Break, Break — 58

Break, break, break — 58

Children, you are very little — 80

Daffodils — 35

Does the road wind uphill all the way? — 67

Eldorado — 64

Escape at Bedtime — 82

Fall, Leaves, Fall — 31

Fall, leaves, fall: die, flowers, away — 31

Faster than fairies, faster than witches — 70

Foreign Lands — 66

For I will consider my cat Jeoffry — 16

Four seasons fill the measure
  of the year — 26

From a Railway Carriage — 70

Full Fathom Five — 52

Full fathom five they father lies — 52

Gaily bedight — 64

Glory be to God for dappled things — 34

Good and Bad Children — 80

He clasps the crag with crooked
  hands — 19

Here a little child I stand — 75

How beautiful is the rain! — 30

How Doth the Little Crocodile — 14

How doth the little crocodile — 14

How Many Miles to Babylon? — 88

How many miles to Babylon? — 88

Hurt No Living Thing — 12

Hurt no living thing — 12

Hush Little Baby — 89

Hush little baby, don't say a word — 89

I have a little shadow that goes in
  and out with me — 36

I met a traveller from an antique land — 62

In winter I get up at night — 84

In Xanadu did Kubla Khan — 44

I Remember, I Remember — 76

I remember, I remember — 76

I Saw a Peacock — 50

I saw a peacock with a fiery tail — 50

I should like to rise and go — 68

I Started Early — 54

I started Early – Took my Dog — 54

Is the Moon Tired? — 85

Is the moon tired? She looks so pale — 85

It's Raining, It's Pouring — 22

It's raining, it's pouring — 22

I wandered lonely as a cloud — 35

Jabberwocky — 10

Kubla Khan — 44

La Belle Dame Sans Merci — 48

Little Orphant Annie — 72

Little Orphant Annie's come to our
  house to stay — 72

Meeting at Night — 60

95

Monday's Child	74
Monday's child is fair of face	74
My Cat Jeoffry	16
My Shadow	36
O Captain! My Captain!	56
O Captain! my Captain! our fearful trip is done	56
O, what can ail thee, knight-at-arms	48
Ozymandias	62
Pied Beauty	34
From Rain in Summer	30
Shall I Compare Thee to a Summer's Day?	41
Shall I compare thee to a summer's day?	41
She Walks in Beauty	40
She walks in beauty, like the night	40
Sleep, Baby, Sleep!	90
Sleep, baby, sleep!	90
Sound the Flute!	29
Spring	29
Star Light, Star Bright	88
Star light, star bright	88
Swing, Swing	78
Swing, swing	78
The Eagle	19
The Ecchoing Green	38
The Fairies	46
The gray sea and the long black land	60
The Herring Loves the Merry Moonlight	15
The herring loves the merry moonlight	15
The Human Seasons	26
The lights from the parlour and kitchen shone out	82
The Maldive Shark	15
The North Wind Doth Blow	24
The north wind doth blow	24
The Owl	18
The Owl and the Pussy-Cat	8
The Owl and the Pussy-Cat went to sea	8
The Rainbow	23
The Silver Swan	19
The silver swan, who living had no note	19
The splendour falls on castle walls	42
The sun does arise	38
The Tyger	20
The Wind	24
The Year's at the Spring	32
The year's at the spring	32
To see a World in a Grain of Sand	12
Travel	68
'Twas brillig, and the slithy toves	10
Tyger! Tyger! burning bright	20
Uphill	67
Up into the cherry-tree	66
Up the airy mountain	46
What Are Heavy?	53
What are heavy? sea-sand and sorrow	53
When cats run home and light is come	18
Whenever the moon and stars are set	25
When icicles hang by the wall	28
Where Lies the Land?	63
Where lies the land to which the ship would go?	63
Whether the Weather Be Fine	22
Whether the weather be fine	22
Who has seen the wind?	24
Windy Nights	25
Winter	28
Wynken, Blynken, and Nod	86
Wynken, Blynken, and Nod one night	86